The Little Book
of
Farmyard Tales

Heather Amery

Illustrated by Stephen Cartwright

Edited by Jenny Tyler
Language Consultant: Betty Root

Cover design by Hannah Ahmed

There is a little yellow duck to find on every page.

PIG GETS STUCK

This is Apple Tree Farm.

This is Mrs. Boot, the farmer. She has two children, called Poppy and Sam, and a dog called Rusty.

On the farm there are six pigs.

The pigs live in a pen with a little house.
The smallest pig is called Curly.

It is time for breakfast.

Mrs. Boot gives the pigs their breakfast.
But Curly is so small, he does not get any.

Curly is hungry.

He looks for something else to eat in the pen.
Then he finds a little gap under the wire.

Curly is out.

He squeezes through the gap under the wire.
He is out in the farmyard.

He meets lots of other animals in the farmyard.
Which breakfast would he like to eat?

Curly wants the hens' breakfast.

He thinks the hens' breakfast looks good.
He squeezes through the gap in the fence.

Curly tries it.

The hens' food is so good, he gobbles it all up.
The hens are not pleased.

Mrs. Boot sees Curly.

Curly hears Mrs. Boot shouting at him.
"What are you doing in the hen run, Curly?"

He runs to the fence.

He tries to squeeze through the gap. But he has
eaten so much breakfast, he is too fat.

Curly is stuck.

Curly pushes and pushes but he can't move.
He is stuck in the fence.

They all push.

Mrs. Boot, Poppy and Sam all push Curly.
He squeals and squeals. His sides hurt.

Curly is out.

Then, with a grunt, Curly pops through the fence.
"He's out, he's out," shouts Sam.

He is safe now.

Mrs. Boot picks up Curly. "Poor little pig," she says. And she carries him back to the pig pen.

Curly is happy.

"Tomorrow you shall have lots of breakfast," she says. And Curly was never, ever hungry again.

THE NAUGHTY SHEEP

This is Apple Tree Farm.

This is Mrs. Boot, the farmer. She has two children, called Poppy and Sam, and a dog called Rusty.

On the farm there are seven sheep.

The sheep live in a big field with a fence around it.
One sheep has a black eye. She is called Woolly.

Woolly is bored.

Woolly stops eating and looks over the fence.
"Grass," she says, "nothing but grass. Boring."

Woolly runs out of the gate.

She runs out of the field into the farmyard. Then she runs through another gate into a garden.

Woolly sees lots to eat in the garden.

She tastes some of the flowers. "Very good,"
she says, "and much prettier than grass."

Can you see where Woolly walked?

She walks around the garden, eating lots of the flowers. "I like flowers," she says.

Mrs. Boot sees Woolly in the garden.

"What are you doing in my garden?" she shouts.
"You've eaten my flowers, you naughty sheep."

Mrs. Boot is very cross.

"It's the Show today," she says. "I was going to pick my best flowers for it. Just look at them."

It is time for the Show.

"Come on," says Poppy. "We must go now. The Show starts soon. It's only just down the road."

They all walk down the road.

Woolly watches them go. She chews her flower and thinks, "I'd like to go to the Show."

Woolly goes to the Show.

Woolly runs down the road. Soon she comes to a
big field with lots of people in it.

Woolly goes into the ring.

She pushes past the people and into the field.
She stops by a man in a white coat.

Mrs. Boot finds her.

"What are you doing here, Woolly?" says Mrs. Boot. "She has just won a prize," says the man.

Woolly is the winner.

"This cup is for the best sheep," says the man.
"Oh, that's lovely. Thank you," says Mrs. Boot.

It is time to go home.

"Come on, Woolly," says Mrs. Boot. "We'll take you back to your field, you naughty, clever sheep."

BARN ON FIRE

This is Apple Tree Farm.

This is Mrs. Boot, the farmer. She has two children, called Poppy and Sam, and a dog called Rusty.

This is Ted.

Ted works at Apple Tree Farm. He looks after the tractor and all the other farm machines.

Poppy and Sam help Ted.

They like helping Ted with jobs on the farm. Today he is fixing the fence around the sheep field.

Sam smells smoke.

"Ted," says Sam, "I think something's burning."
Ted stops working and they all sniff hard.

The barn is on fire.

"Look," says Poppy, "there's smoke coming from the hay barn. It must be on fire. What shall we do?"

"Call a fire engine."

"Come on," says Ted. "Run to the house. We must call a fire engine. Run as fast as you can."

Poppy and Sam run to the house.

"Help!" shouts Poppy. "Call a fire engine.
Quickly! The hay barn is on fire."

Mrs. Boot dials the number.

"It's Apple Tree Farm," she says. "A fire engine please, as fast as you can. Thank you very much."

"You must stay here."

"Now, Poppy," says Mrs. Boot. "I want you and
Sam to stay indoors. And don't let Rusty out."

Poppy and Sam watch from the door.

Soon they hear the siren. Then the fire engine
roars up the road and into the farmyard.

"The firemen are here."

The firemen jump down from the engine.
They lift down lots of hoses and unroll them.

The firemen run over to the barn with the hoses.
Can you see where they get the water from?

The firemen squirt water onto the barn.

Poppy and Sam watch them from the window. "It's still burning on the other side," says Poppy.

"There's the fire."

One fireman runs behind the barn. What a surprise!
Two campers are cooking on a big wood fire.

The fire is out.

"We're sorry," say the campers. "It was exciting," says Sam, "but I'm glad the barn is all right."

THE RUNAWAY TRACTOR

This is Apple Tree Farm.

This is Mrs. Boot, the farmer. She has two children, called Poppy and Sam, and a dog called Rusty.

Ted is the tractor driver.

He has filled the trailer with hay. He is taking it to the fields to feed the sheep.

Poppy and Sam hear a funny noise.

"Listen," says Sam. "Ted is shouting and the tractor is making a funny noise. Let's go and look."

They run to the top of the hill.

The tractor is racing down the hill, going faster and faster. "It won't stop," shouts Ted.

The trailer comes off.

The trailer runs down the hill and crashes into a fence. It tips up and all the hay falls out.

The tractor runs into the pond.

The tractor hits the water with a great splash. The engine makes a loud noise, then it stops with a hiss.

Ted climbs down from the tractor.

Ted paddles through the water and out of the pond. Poppy and Sam run down the hill.

Ted is very wet.

Ted takes off his boots and tips out the water.
How can he get the tractor out of the pond?

"Go and ask Farmer Dray to help."

"Ask someone to telephone Farmer Dray," says Ted. Poppy and Sam run off to the house.

Farmer Dray has a big horse.

Soon he walks down the hill with his horse.
It is a huge carthorse, called Dolly.

Ted helps with the ropes.

Farmer Dray ties the ropes to the horse. Ted ties the other ends to the tractor.

Dolly pulls and pulls.

Very slowly the tractor starts to move. Ted pushes as hard as he can and Dolly pulls.

Ted falls over.

The tractor jerks forward and Ted falls in the water. Now he is wet and muddy all over.

The tractor is out of the pond.

"Better leave the tractor to dry," says Farmer Dray. "Then you can get the engine going again."

Poppy and Sam ride home.

Farmer Dray lifts them onto Dolly's back.
But Ted is so muddy, he has to walk.

PIG GETS
LOST

This is Apple Tree Farm.

This is Mrs. Boot, the farmer. She has two children, called Poppy and Sam, and a dog called Rusty.

Mrs. Boot has six pigs.

There is a mother pig and five baby pigs. The
smallest pig is called Curly. They live in a pen.

Mrs. Boot feeds the pigs every morning.

She takes them two big buckets of food.
But where is Curly? He is not in the pen.

She calls Poppy and Sam.

"Curly's gone," she says. "I need your help to find him."

"Where are you, Curly?"

Poppy and Sam call to Curly. "Let's look in the hen run," says Mrs. Boot. But Curly is not there.

"There he is, in the barn."

"He's in the barn," says Sam. "I can just see his tail." They all run into the barn to catch Curly.

71

"That's not Curly."

"It's only a piece of rope," says Mrs. Boot. "Not Curly's tail." "Where can he be?" says Poppy.

"Maybe he's eating the cows' food."

But Curly is not with the cows. "Don't worry," says Mrs. Boot. "We'll soon find him."

"Perhaps he's in the garden."

They look for Curly in the garden, but he is not there. "We'll never find him," says Sam.

"Why is Rusty barking?"

Rusty is standing by a ditch. He barks and barks.
"He's trying to tell us something," says Poppy.

"Rusty has found Curly."

They all look in the ditch. Curly has slipped down into the mud and can't climb out.

"We'll have to lift him out."

"I'll get into the ditch," says Mrs. Boot. "I'm coming too," says Poppy. "And me," says Sam.

Curly is very muddy.

Mrs. Boot picks Curly up but he struggles. Then he slips back into the mud with a splash.

Now everyone is very muddy.

Sam tries to catch Curly but he falls into the mud.
Mrs. Boot grabs Curly and climbs out of the ditch.

They all climb out of the ditch.

"We all need a good bath," says Mrs. Boot.
"Rusty found Curly. Clever dog," says Sam.

THE HUNGRY DONKEY

This is Apple Tree Farm.

This is Mrs. Boot, the farmer. She has two children, called Poppy and Sam, and a dog called Rusty.

There is a donkey on the farm.

The donkey is called Ears. She lives in a field with lots of grass, but she is always hungry.

Ears, the donkey, is going out.

Poppy and Sam catch Ears and take her to the farmyard. Today is the day of the Show.

Ears has a little cart.

They brush her coat, comb her tail and clean her feet. Mrs. Boot puts her into her little cart.

Off they go to the Show.

Poppy and Sam climb up into the little cart. They all go down the lane to the show ground.

"You stay here, Ears."

At the show ground, Mrs. Boot ties Ears to a fence. "Stay here. We'll be back soon," she says.

Ears gets free.

Ears is hungry and bored with nothing to do.
She pulls and pulls on the rope until she is free.

Ears looks for food.

Ears trots across the field to the show ring.
She sees a bunch of flowers and some fruit.

"That looks good to eat."

She takes a big bite, but the flowers do not taste very nice. A lady screams and Ears is frightened.

90

Ears runs away.

Mrs. Boot, Poppy and Sam and the lady run after her and catch her.

"Naughty donkey," says Sam.

"I'm sorry," Mrs. Boot says to the lady. "Would you like to take Ears into the best donkey competition?"

Ears is very good now.

The lady is called Mrs. Rose. She climbs into the cart. "Come on," she says, and shakes the reins.

Ears pulls the cart into the show ring.

She trots in front of the judges. She stops and goes when Mrs. Rose tells her.

Ears wins a prize.

"Well done," says the judge, giving her a rosette.
He gives Mrs. Rose a prize too. It is a hat.

It is time to go home.

Mrs. Rose waves goodbye. "That was such fun," she says. Ears trots home. She has a new hat too.

SCARECROW'S SECRET

This is Apple Tree Farm.

This is Mrs. Boot, the farmer. She has two children, called Poppy and Sam, and a dog called Rusty.

Mr. Boot is working in the barn.

"What are you doing, Dad?" asks Sam. "I'm tying lots of straw on these poles," says Mr. Boot.

"What is it?"

"You'll soon see," says Mr. Boot. "Go and get my old coat from the shed, please. Bring my old hat too."

"It's going to be a scarecrow."

Poppy and Sam come back with the coat and hat.
Then they help Mr. Boot put them on the scarecrow.

"He's just like a nice old man."

"I've got some old gloves for him," says Sam.
"Let's call him Mr. Straw," says Poppy.

"He's finished now."

"Help me carry him, please, Poppy," says
Mr. Boot. "You bring the spade, Sam."

They all go to the cornfield.

Mr. Boot digs a hole in the field. Then he pushes in the pole so that Mr. Straw stands up.

"He does look real."

"I'm sure Mr. Straw will scare off all the birds,"
says Sam. "Especially the crows," says Poppy.

Mr. Straw is doing a good job.

Every day Mr. Boot, Poppy and Sam look at
Mr. Straw. There are no birds in the cornfield.

"There's Farmer Dray's scarecrow."

"He's no good at all," says Sam. "The birds are eating all the corn and standing on the scarecrow."

"Why is Mr. Straw so good?"

"Sometimes he looks as if he is moving," says Poppy. "His coat goes up and down. It's very odd."

"Let's go and look."

"Let's creep up very quietly," says Sam. And they tiptoe across the cornfield to look at Mr. Straw.

"There's something inside his coat."

"It's moving," says Poppy. "And it's making a funny noise. What is it?" says Sam.

"It's our cat and her kittens."

Carefully they open the coat. There is Whiskers, the cat, and two baby kittens hiding in the straw.

111

"So that's the scarecrow's secret."

"Whiskers is helping Mr. Straw to frighten off the birds," says Poppy. "Clever Mr. Straw," says Sam.

TRACTOR IN TROUBLE

This is Apple Tree Farm.

This is Mrs. Boot, the farmer. She has two children, called Poppy and Sam, and a dog called Rusty.

Ted works on the farm.

He helps Mrs. Boot. Ted looks after the tractor
and all the farm machines.

Today it is very windy.

The wind is blowing the trees and it is very cold.
Poppy and Sam play in the barn.

"Where are you going, Ted?"

Ted is driving the tractor out of the yard. "I'm just going to see if the sheep are all right," he says.

Ted stops the tractor by the gate.

He goes into the sheep field. He nails down
the roof of the sheep shed to make it safe.

Poppy and Sam hear a terrible crash.

"What's that?" says Sam. "I don't know. Let's go and look," says Poppy. They run down the field.

"A tree has blown down."

"It's coming down on Ted's tractor," says Poppy.
"Come on. We must help him," says Sam.

"What are you going to do, Ted?"

Poor Ted is very upset. The tree has scratched his new tractor. He can't even get into the cab.

"Ask Farmer Dray to help."

"I think I can see him on the hill," says Ted.
Poppy and Sam run to ask him.

Soon Farmer Dray comes with his horse.

Farmer Dray has a big, gentle carthorse, called Dolly. They have come to help Ted.

"I'll cut up the tree first."

Farmer Dray starts up his chain saw. Then he cuts off the branches which have fallen on the tractor.

Dolly starts to work.

Farmer Dray ties two ropes to Dolly's harness.
Ted ties the other ends to the big branches.

Dolly pulls and pulls.

She works hard until all the branches are off the tractor. "Well done, Dolly," says Farmer Dray.

Ted climbs up into the cab.

"Thank you very much, Farmer Dray and Dolly,"
he says. And they all go back to the farmyard.

127

The tractor looks a little messy.

Ted finds a brush and paints over all the scratches.
"It will soon be as good as new," he says.

THE SILLY
SHEEPDOG

This is Apple Tree Farm.

This is Mrs. Boot, the farmer. She has two children, called Poppy and Sam, and a dog called Rusty.

Ted works on Apple Tree Farm.

He has just bought a sheepdog to help him with the sheep. The sheepdog is called Patch.

Poppy, Sam and Rusty say hello to Patch.

"Come on, Patch," says Sam. "We'll show you all the animals on our farm."

First they look at the hens.

Patch jumps into the hen run and chases the hens.
They are frightened and fly up onto their house.

"Now we'll go and see the cows."

Patch runs into the field and barks at the cows.
But they just stand and stare at him.

Then they look at the pigs.

Patch jumps into the pig pen and chases all the pigs into their little house.

Sam shouts at Patch.

"Come here, you silly thing. You're meant to be a sheepdog. Ted will have to send you back."

They go to the sheep field.

"Look," says Sam. "One sheep is missing." "Yes, it's that naughty Woolly again," says Ted.

"Where's Patch going?" says Sam.

Patch runs away across the field. Ted, Sam,
Poppy and Rusty run after him.

Patch dives through the hedge.

Patch barks and barks. "What has he found?" says Sam. They all go to look.

Patch has found a boy.

The boy pats Patch. "Hello," he says. "I wondered who bought you when my dad sold his farm."

The boy has found a sheep.

"There's Woolly," says Sam. "I found her on the road," says the boy. "I was bringing her back."

The boy whistles to Patch.

Patch chases Woolly back through the gate. She runs into the field with the other sheep.

Ted stares in surprise.

"Patch doesn't do anything I tell him," says Ted.
"You don't know how to whistle," says the boy.

Patch runs back to them.

"You must teach me how to whistle to Patch,"
says Ted. "He's not a silly dog after all," says Sam.

KITTEN'S
DAY OUT

This is Apple Tree Farm.

This is Mrs. Boot, the farmer. She has two children, called Poppy and Sam, and a dog called Rusty.

Ted works on the farm.

He is helping Mr. Bran, the truck driver. Mr. Bran has brought some sacks of food for the cows.

They say goodbye to Mr. Bran.

Mr. Bran waves as he drives his truck out of the farmyard. Ted and Poppy wave back.

148

"Where's my kitten?"

"Where's Fluff?" says Sam. They all look everywhere for Fluff. But they can't find her.

"Perhaps she jumped on the truck."

"Take my car and go after the truck, Ted," says
Mrs. Boot. They jump in the car and drive off.

Ted stops the car at the crossroads.

"Which way did Mr. Bran go?" says Ted. "There's a truck," says Sam. "It's just going around the bend."

Ted drives down a steep hill.

"Look out Ted," says Poppy. There's a stream at the bottom. The car splashes into the water.

The car stops in the stream.

"Water in the engine," says Ted. "I'll have to push." "We'll never find the truck now," says Sam.

Ted looks inside the car.

He mops up all the water. Soon he gets the car to start again. They drive on to look for the truck.

There are lots of sheep on the road.

"The sheep came out of the field. Someone left the gate open," says Ted. "We must get them back."

Ted, Poppy and Sam round up the sheep.

They drive them back into the field. Ted shuts the gate. "Come on, we must hurry," says Sam.

"Stop, Ted, there's a truck."

"I'm sure that's Mr. Bran's truck in that farmyard,"
says Sam. Ted drives in to see.

"It's the wrong truck."

"Oh dear," says Poppy. "It's not Mr. Bran, and that's not Mr. Bran's truck."

Ted drives them home.

"We'll never find my kitten now," says Sam.
"I'm sure she'll turn up," says Poppy.

There's a surprise at Apple Tree Farm.

"Here's your kitten," says Mr. Bran. "She's been in my truck all day and now I've brought her home."

This edition first published in 2002 by Usborne Publishing Ltd., Usborne House, 83-85 Saffron Hill, London EC1N 8RT, England. www.usborne.com Copyright © 2002, 2000, 1999, 1996, 1995, 1992, 1990, 1989 Usborne Publishing Ltd.